Poll
Pon

Be
Blackcurrant

Alice Apple

Peter
Potato

Grace Grape

Wee Willie
Water Melon

The Garden Gang
Stories and pictures by
Jayne Fisher

Other Garden Gang stories

Series 793

© LADYBIRD BOOKS LTD MCMLXXXIII

All rights reserved. No part of this publication may be reproduced, stored in a retrieval system, or transmitted in any form or by any means, electronic, mechanical, photocopying, recording or otherwise, without the prior consent of the copyright owner.

Pedro Pepper

Ladybird Books Loughborough

Pedro Pepper sat
by his little fire
and shivered.
He not only shivered,
he also looked
extremely miserable.
A huge shawl was
draped around his
shoulders and
there was a hot cup
of cocoa beside him.
But he could not
get warm.

Pedro had only been
living in the garden
for three months.
He had always wanted
to visit Britain,
so being the
adventurous type
he had travelled from
Mexico, all by himself,
on a huge boat.
When he had arrived
in the garden it was
warm and sunny.

Now Pedro could not
understand why
it had become
so cold.
The sky was grey and
everything looked so
bleak and bare.
"Where have the bees
and butterflies gone?"
thought Pedro.
"And why don't
the birds sing
any more?"
A large tear ran down
his face.

He went over
to the window.
Perhaps he might see
some of his friends
in the garden.
But oh dear me!
Something very strange
had happened
to the glass.
It had a beautiful
feathery pattern
all over it and
he certainly couldn't
see out.
He was more
and more puzzled.

Again Pedro shivered
and, taking his
big shawl and a
hot water bottle,
he crept up to bed.
"I shall never be
really warm again,"
he thought, sadly.
He was soon fast
asleep and as he
slept he dreamed of
the hot Mexican
sunshine and the
jolly friends he had
left behind.

It was late
when he awoke
and he could hear
squeals and laughter
in the garden.
He hurried over
to the window.
Pedro rubbed the
glass and was very
surprised to find that
the feathery pattern
melted away under
his hand.
His fingers were
wet and cold as he
peered through the
clear patch.

What a sight met his
eyes. "I must be
dreaming," he thought.
Falling from the sky were
millions and millions
of white feathers,
floating gently
downwards, covering
the houses, the trees
and the earth.
Everything everywhere
was dazzling white.
Suddenly a sunbeam
shone through a cloud
and everything sparkled.

"How beautiful,"
thought Pedro.
Quite suddenly he
had forgotten the cold.
All the Garden Gang
were out there,
shouting and laughing.
Some were throwing
the feathers around,
others were sliding or
pulling each other along
on strange contraptions.
Many of the younger
Garden Gang were
building peculiar
white men with funny
hats.

19

Alice Apple was the first
to miss Pedro.
As you know,
she was always
laughing and singing and
because Pedro was
usually so cheerful and
jolly she had become
one of his best friends.
She looked towards
his house and saw
him looking through
the window.
She waved to him
and asked him
to come out.

Poor Pedro.
He shook his head
and looked quite scared.
"Please come out,"
they all cried together.
"We're having such
great fun."
"Oh, I couldn't possibly
come out there,"
shouted Pedro.
"It's much too cold.
Besides all those
feathers will only make
me sneeze."

How they all roared with
laughter. "These aren't
feathers, it's snow!"
they shouted.
"And the pattern
on your window
is called frost. The best
way to stop shivering is
to come out and play!"
So Pedro put on a warm
scarf and gloves and
went out to play.
And do you know,
for the first time that
winter he found
that he was . . .

really
warm!

The
Cherry Twins

Charlie and Cheryl were
cheerful little cherries.
Both were full of fun
and chatter and were
never apart.
They were twins
you see. They did
everything together.
They even spoke at
the same time.
But their favourite
pastime was hiding:
hiding in corners, behind
trees, under tables,
in fact, anywhere.

Mr and Mrs Cherry
loved their little twins
very much and
sometimes worried
a great deal
when they had been
searching for the
mischievous pair.
They would look
in all the usual
hiding places
but Charlie and Cheryl
always seemed to find
a new place to hide.

Once when Mrs Cherry
took the twins
to visit Roger Radish
he made them all
a pot of tea.
Afterwards Mrs Cherry
insisted on doing the
washing up and
while she was busy
you can guess what
happened can't you?
That's right!
The twins disappeared.
Roger said, "Don't worry.
I'll soon find them."

He searched upstairs
and downstairs.
They were not there.
He went outside
and began to search
in the garden.
They were not behind
the compost heap.
They were not under
the flower pots.
They were not behind
the greenhouse.
"They're here," called
Roger, as he spied the
twins crouching behind
the rockery.

"Cheryl and Charlie
are becoming quite a
problem," said Mrs
Cherry to Mr Cherry
one evening, when the
twins were tucked up
safely in bed.
"One of these days,
they will be lost
for ever. I do wish
they wouldn't hide.
Today I spent hours
looking for them."

Many of the neighbours
suggested ideas for
keeping them safe,
but nothing seemed
to work.
Tobias Turnip thought
they should be
kept in a giant play-pen
all day, but they were
much too old for that
sort of thing.
The twins enjoyed
hiding and couldn't
understand what the
fuss was about.

39

Gertrude Gooseberry
arranged for
the Garden Gang
to take it in turns
to watch the twins
while Mrs Cherry
got on with her
housework.
Even that didn't work.
Those naughty twins
somehow managed
to slip away and hide.
Once it took half
a day to find them.

41

It was coming up
to the twins' fourth
birthday and
Mr and Mrs Cherry
decided to give
them a big surprise
birthday party.
They would invite
all the Garden Gang
and make a very
special tea.
Perhaps if they gave
the twins this
wonderful treat they
would stop hiding.

How Mrs Cherry
managed to get the
party ready I really
don't know,
because most of the
week was spent in
looking for the twins.
She baked pies,
sausage rolls,
bread and cakes.
She made jellies and
ginger pop and even
made some ice cream.
All this, she managed
to keep secret.

FLOUR

45

The twins' birthday
came at last
and everyone was
looking forward
to the party.
Charlie and Cheryl
were dressed in
their best clothes and
the guests began
to arrive.
"Time for tea!"
called Mrs Cherry.
But where were
the twins?
Everyone began to
search and Mrs
Cherry began to cry.

GINGER
POP

For hours they searched
and soon it began
to grow dark.
"Why do they hide?"
wept Mrs Cherry.
Suddenly a smiling
Peter Potato appeared
with the tearful twins
in his arms.
They had gone to
hide in his shed
and accidentally
got locked in.
Everyone had a wonderful
party after that
and do you know,
Charlie and Cheryl . . .

never hid again!

Paul Pumpkin

Bertie Brussels Sprout

Mark Marrow

Gertru
Gooseber

Tim Tomato

Patrick Pear

Avril Apricot